Adapted by Erica David

Illustrated by Fabio Laguna and Patrick Spaziante

🌻 A GOLDEN BOOK • NEW YORK

randomhouse.com/kids
ISBN 978-0-385-37142-1
Printed in the United States of America
10 9 8 7 6 5 4 3 2 1

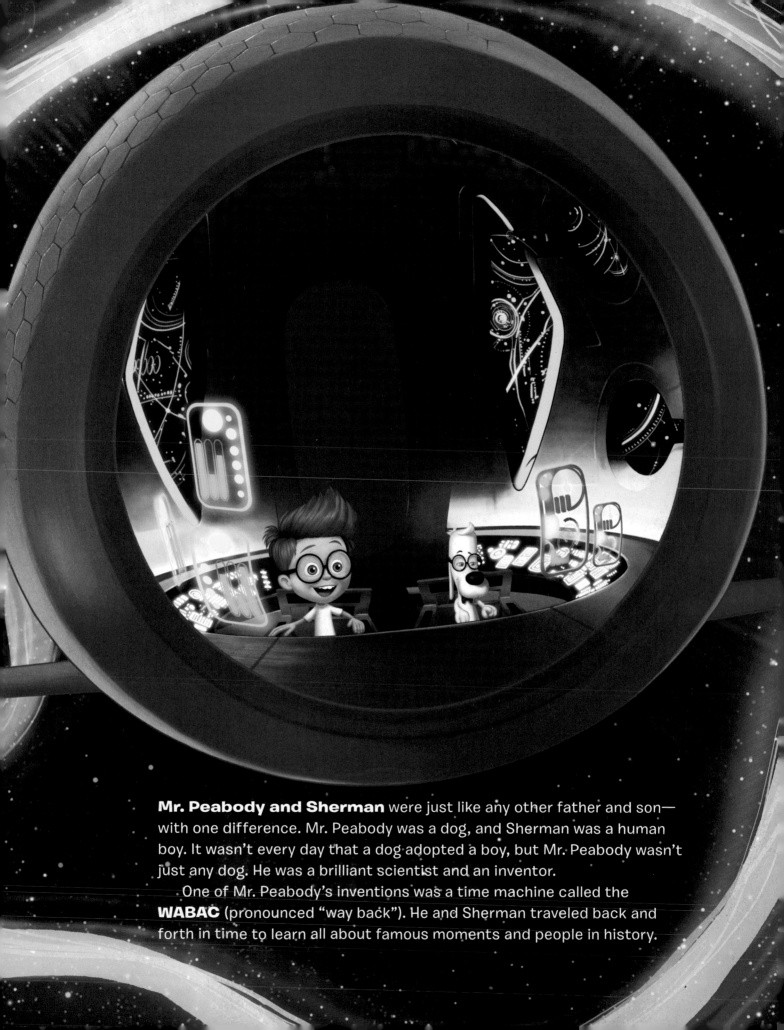

Mr. Peabody and Sherman were just like any other father and son—with one difference. Mr. Peabody was a dog, and Sherman was a human boy. It wasn't every day that a dog adopted a boy, but Mr. Peabody wasn't just any dog. He was a brilliant scientist and an inventor.

One of Mr. Peabody's inventions was a time machine called the **WABAC** (pronounced "way back"). He and Sherman traveled back and forth in time to learn all about famous moments and people in history.

On one trip to the past, Mr. Peabody and Sherman traveled to the year 1789 to learn about the **French Revolution**. They visited the French queen, Marie Antoinette, in her fancy castle.

Mr. Peabody warned Sherman to stay close. He explained, "Marie Antoinette's expensive tastes made her the target of much criticism."

As usual, Mr. Peabody was right. Outside the castle, a group of peasants gathered. They were very poor and very hungry. When the peasants heard the queen say, "**Let zem eat cake**," they got angry. The queen and her rich friends were eating cake while the poor had nothing!

Led by a man named **Robespierre**, the angry peasants stormed the castle. Mr. Peabody was the first to be captured. They took him to the guillotine to chop off his head!

But with clever thinking, Mr. Peabody tricked Robespierre and escaped with Sherman.

Robespierre and his guards chased Mr. Peabody and Sherman through the sewers of Paris. During a daring sword fight, Mr. Peabody struck a water pipe.

"Ha! You missed," Robespierre sneered.

"I never miss," Mr. Peabody replied as the pipe burst, flooding the sewer. Mr. Peabody and Sherman surfed to freedom on a giant wave!

As with all of Mr. Peabody's lessons, Sherman would never forget what he learned about the French Revolution!

Back in the present, it was Sherman's first day of school. Mr. Peabody was excited for his boy, but a little worried, too. School was one adventure Sherman would have to face on his own.

Mr. Peabody gave Sherman a special dog whistle to use if he ever needed help. Sherman tucked the whistle into his pocket and ran into the school. He couldn't wait to get to class!

That morning, Sherman's class had a history lesson about George Washington. As soon as the teacher asked a question, Sherman raised his hand. He knew all about George Washington from his trips in the WABAC. One student, **Penny Peterson**, got mad that Sherman knew all the answers. She was used to being the best student in her class. Now she had competition.

At lunch, Penny was mean to Sherman. First she threw his sandwich on the ground. Then she grabbed his special dog whistle and wouldn't give it back to him. Sherman did his best to ignore her . . . until she said, "Your dad is a dog, **so you're a dog, too**."

Sherman finally lost his temper.

"Fight! Fight! Fight!" the other students yelled as Sherman and Penny wrestled for the whistle.

Later, Mr. Peabody was called to Principal Purdy's office. The principal told him that Sherman had bitten Penny! The incident had been reported to the Bureau of Child Safety and Protection.

A woman named Miss Grunion came to investigate. She thought Sherman's bad behavior was Mr. Peabody's fault. "After all, you are a dog," she sneered. Miss Grunion gave Mr. Peabody a warning: if Penny's parents pressed charges, she would take Sherman away from him.

Sherman apologized for fighting with Penny, but Mr. Peabody was still worried. What if Penny's parents pressed charges? He could lose Sherman **forever**!

Mr. Peabody couldn't let that happen. He scratched his chin, deep in thought. Suddenly, he got an idea!

The next day, Mr. Peabody invited Penny and her parents over for dinner. "We're so delighted you could make it on such short notice," he told them. He wanted to make friends with them—and he wanted Sherman to make friends with Penny.

But Sherman didn't want to spend any more time with Penny than he had to. He knew she hated him! Reluctantly, he took Penny to his room while Mr. Peabody talked to her parents.

Mr. Peabody tried his best to impress Paul and Patty Peterson. He cooked a fancy meal, told funny stories, and played songs on different instruments.

Patty was delighted, but Paul wasn't convinced—until Mr. Peabody fixed his **bad** back!

Meanwhile, Penny asked Sherman how he knew so much about history. Sherman didn't answer. Mr. Peabody had warned him, "Don't tell anyone about the WABAC."

But Penny kept pestering Sherman until he finally let it slip that he had actually talked to George Washington. Sherman groaned. Now he would have to tell her **everything**!

In the living room, Mr. Peabody had completely charmed the Petersons. They were not going to press charges. Mr. Peabody's plan was a success!

Just then, Sherman came in and pulled Mr. Peabody aside. He confessed that he had used the time machine and accidentally lost Penny in **ancient Egypt**!

To keep Penny's parents from finding out what had happened, Mr. Peabody used hypnosis to put them into a trance.

Mr. Peabody and Sherman raced to the WABAC and set a course for ancient Egypt. They had to find Penny and bring her back to the present before her parents woke up!

"That's not going to be easy," Sherman told Mr. Peabody. "She's **impossible**!"

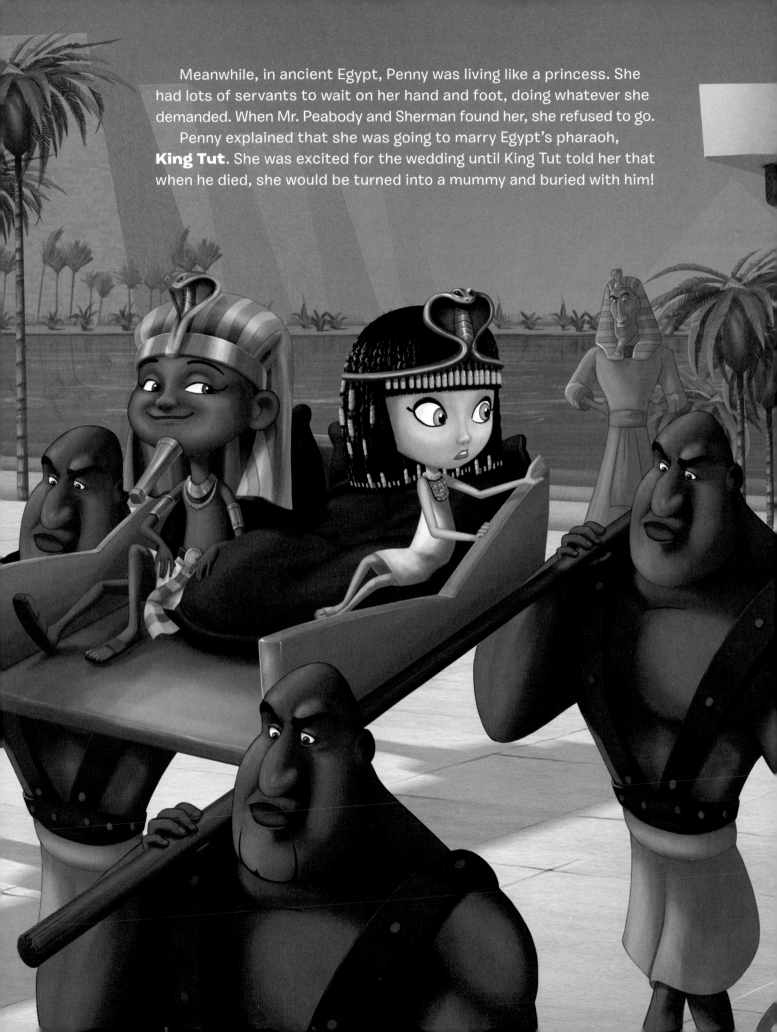

Meanwhile, in ancient Egypt, Penny was living like a princess. She had lots of servants to wait on her hand and foot, doing whatever she demanded. When Mr. Peabody and Sherman found her, she refused to go. Penny explained that she was going to marry Egypt's pharaoh, **King Tut**. She was excited for the wedding until King Tut told her that when he died, she would be turned into a mummy and buried with him!

YUCK! That made Penny change her mind. Now she wanted to leave with Mr. Peabody and Sherman, but King Tut wouldn't let her.

"Don't worry," Sherman told her as Tut's guards dragged him and Mr. Peabody away. "We'll save you."

Mr. Peabody and Sherman were thrown into a **dark tomb**. Mr. Peabody immediately began looking for a way to escape. He discovered a secret passage that led to a pair of boats. Mr. Peabody read the hieroglyphics carved into the stone walls. One boat would take them to the tomb's exit, but the other would take the rider to his or her doom!

Mr. Peabody quickly figured out how to set the boats in motion, but Sherman jumped into the wrong one. At the last minute, Mr. Peabody swung on a rope and pulled Sherman to safety. Their boat sailed into the air and carried them out of the tomb.

Later, Penny's wedding to King Tut was under way. But a loud voice interrupted the ceremony: **"This wedding must not continue!"**

Everyone looked up at the giant statue of the Egyptian god Anubis. They couldn't believe their eyes. The statue was talking!

Inside the statue, Mr. Peabody and Sherman were pretending to be Anubis.

The statue ordered King Tut to release Penny, and the crowd cried out, "The girl must go!"

Suddenly, there was a loud crack! The statue's mouth broke open. Mr. Peabody, Sherman, and the jaw came crashing down. When King Tut realized he'd been tricked, he and his guards dashed after Penny, Sherman, and Mr. Peabody. Luckily, the three of them escaped and made it safely to the WABAC.

On board the WABAC, Mr. Peabody discovered a problem: there wasn't enough power for the trip home. He told Sherman and Penny they'd have to stop during the Renaissance and visit his old friend, the artist and inventor **Leonardo da Vinci**. The painter was happy to help.

The two geniuses quickly got to work fixing the
WABAC. Sherman tried to help, but he kept getting in
the way. So Mr. Peabody let Sherman go play with Penny.

Sherman found Penny staring at one of Leonardo's inventions: a flying machine. She tricked Sherman into taking the machine for a ride.

Sherman was terrified as they flew over the city. **"This is crazy!"** he shouted.

"It's fun!" Penny replied.

At first, Sherman was afraid to pilot the machine, but when Penny let go of the controls, he had no choice. "**You can do it**, Sherman!" she said. Sherman swallowed his fear and soared.

Mr. Peabody and Leonardo had just finished fixing the WABAC when they spotted Sherman and Penny in the flying machine. Mr. Peabody frowned. Sherman didn't have his permission to fly!

Mr. Peabody ordered Sherman to come down immediately, which caused the boy to lose concentration. The kids crashed into a tree! Mr. Peabody was glad no one was hurt, but he was still angry. Everyone else thought it was fantastic. Leonardo said, "Sherman, you are the first flying man!"

Later, Mr. Peabody and Sherman argued in the WABAC. Penny took Sherman's side, asking his father, "If you're such a great parent, then why is Miss Grunion trying to take Sherman away from you?"

Sherman was shocked. Why hadn't Mr. Peabody told him? He was fed up with the way Mr. Peabody treated him. **"I'm not a dog,"** he said.

Mr. Peabody tried to explain, but suddenly a powerful black hole appeared. Even with Mr. Peabody's quick thinking, the WABAC barely escaped!

When the WABAC landed, Sherman ran away. Mr. Peabody and Penny searched all over for him. Finally, they came to a giant wooden horse outside the gates of a walled city. Mr. Peabody's eyes widened as he realized they were in the middle of the **Trojan War**, an ancient conflict between Greece and Troy!

Mr. Peabody and Penny found Sherman hiding inside the horse with some Greek soldiers. He had joined the Greek army! Mr. Peabody tried to convince the soldiers that Sherman was too young to join them in battle. But Sherman and his new Greek brothers disagreed.

The city gates opened, and the wooden horse was pulled inside. The Greek soldiers leapt out of the horse and attacked the city. Sherman was caught in the middle of the battle! Luckily, Mr. Peabody came to his rescue.

Mr. Peabody, Sherman, and Penny fled the battle in the wooden horse as it barreled out of the city. Unfortunately, there was a cliff ahead! Mr. Peabody used a rope and a grappling hook to snag a section of the city wall. He stopped the horse, but it teetered **dangerously** over the edge of the cliff.

Mr. Peabody got Sherman and Penny to safety. Then, before Mr. Peabody could get out, the horse slipped off the cliff and crashed to the rocks below!

"Mr. Peabody!" Sherman wailed.

"What are we going to do?" Penny said.

Sherman had an idea. "The only **person**
who can help us *is* Mr. Peabody!" he explained.
They would use the WABAC to travel in time
back to the dinner party and ask *that* Mr.
Peabody what to do! Sherman and Penny
raced to the WABAC and blasted off.
        They didn't see Mr. Peabody.
He was alive!

When Sherman and Penny arrived at the dinner party, they pulled Mr. Peabody aside and told him everything. "What should we do?" Sherman asked. But before Mr. Peabody could answer, the other Sherman appeared, saying he'd lost Penny in ancient Egypt. Now there were **two** Shermans!

"Don't get too close!" Mr. Peabody warned. "It's putting too much **strain** on the space-time continuum!"

While Mr. Peabody came up with a plan to set things right, the other Mr. Peabody showed up. "How did you get back?" Sherman asked, relieved to see his dad. This Mr. Peabody told them that he had built a time machine with bone and yak fat—and it had worked perfectly!

Meanwhile, **Miss Grunion** arrived for a surprise inspection. When she saw the two Shermans and two Mr. Peabodys, her suspicions were confirmed: Mr. Peabody was a bad parent!

"I've seen quite enough to remove the boy—both boys—from this home!" said Miss Grunion.

Miss Grunion grabbed both Shermans, but as they tried to break free, they crashed into each other and morphed together! Both Mr. Peabodys tried to break them up . . . but all four of them morphed together instead! Suddenly, they turned back into one Sherman and one Mr. Peabody—but the time line was ruined! It was only a matter of time before all **history** went haywire.

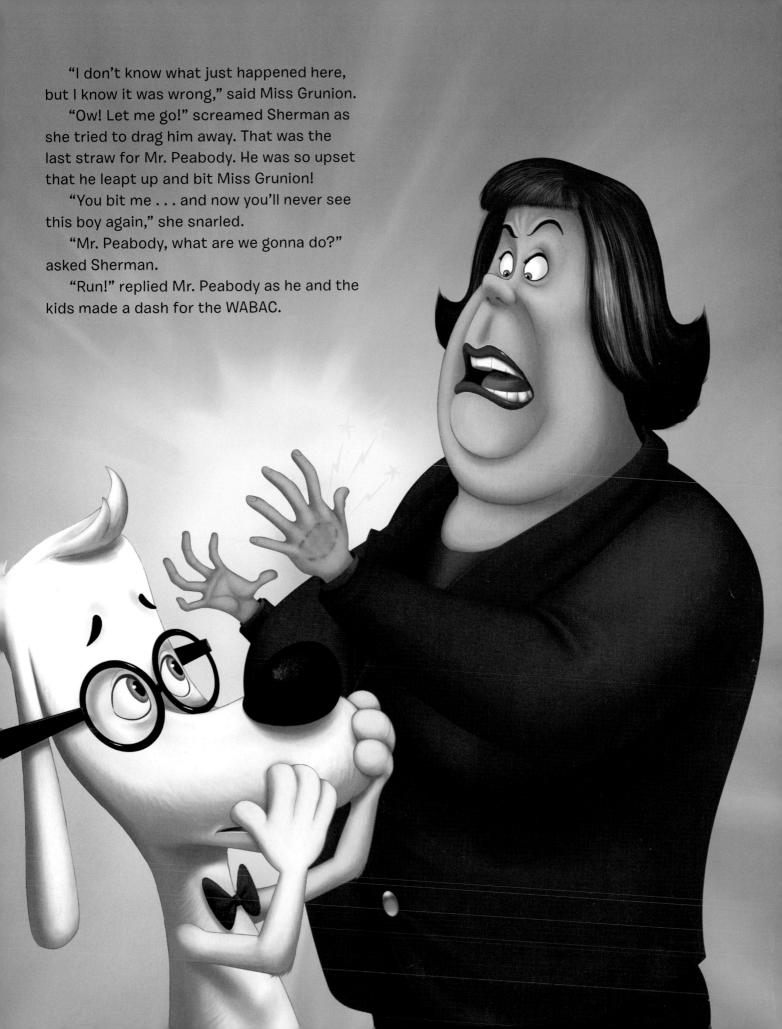

"I don't know what just happened here, but I know it was wrong," said Miss Grunion.

"Ow! Let me go!" screamed Sherman as she tried to drag him away. That was the last straw for Mr. Peabody. He was so upset that he leapt up and bit Miss Grunion!

"You bit me . . . and now you'll never see this boy again," she snarled.

"Mr. Peabody, what are we gonna do?" asked Sherman.

"Run!" replied Mr. Peabody as he and the kids made a dash for the WABAC.

Mr. Peabody, Sherman, and Penny blasted off in the WABAC, but they couldn't find a wormhole to time-travel through!

"We need to get to the past and erase this mess," said Mr. Peabody.

"Looks like the past is coming to us!" replied Sherman as famous people from history ran through the streets of New York!

The WABAC landed in Central Park just as Miss Grunion arrived with the police.

"Mr. Peabody, you're under arrest for reckless endangerment!" an officer shouted.

"This is what happens when you let a dog adopt a boy," added Miss Grunion. "Take him away!"

This gave Sherman an **idea**.

If being a dog meant that he was like Mr. Peabody—who was always there to help, and who loved him no matter what—then he was proud to be a dog. "I'm a dog, too!" he declared.

Soon everyone from Robespierre to King Tut to Leonardo da Vinci—and even Penny—began to shout, "I'm a dog, too!"

George Washington declared that it was perfectly fine for a boy and a dog to be a family. "I hereby award Mr. Peabody a presidential pardon," he said.

Mr. Peabody and Sherman had one thing left to do:
fix all of time! They climbed into the WABAC—but for
once Mr. Peabody wasn't sure what to do.
"Why not go to the future?" Sherman suggested.
"It's probably not all screwed up."

"You're a genius!" Mr. Peabody declared. He was so
proud of his son that he let him drive. "I love you, Sherman."
Sherman smiled as the WABAC took off with a **boom**!
The future looked bright.

Sherman's idea worked, and everything returned to normal. But it was only the beginning of Mr. Peabody, Sherman, and Penny's adventures.